Zoey
AND
SASSAFRAS
BIPS AND ROSES

READ THE REST OF THE SERIES

for activities and more visit
ZOEYANDSASSAFRAS.COM

TABLE OF CONTENTS

FOR CHLOE, LYRA, AMELIA, OSCAR,
AVA, AND OF COURSE, NINA! — ML
FOR BUBS AND GOOSE! — AC

Audience: Grades K-5.
LCCN 2020935939
ISBN 9781943147809; ISBN 9781943147816; ISBN 9781943147823

Text copyright 2020 by Asia Citro
Illustrations copyright 2020 by Marion Lindsay
Journal entries handwritten by S. Citro

Published by The Innovation Press
1001 4th Avenue, Suite 3200 Seattle, WA 98154
www.theinnovationpress.com

Printed and bound by Worzalla
Production Date: August 2020 | Plant Location: Stevens Point, Wisconsin

Cover design by Nicole LaRue | Book layout by Kerry Ellis

PROLOGUE

These days my cat Sassafras and I are always desperately hoping we'll hear our barn doorbell.

I know most people are excited to hear their doorbell ring. It might mean a present or package delivery, or a friend showing up to play. But our doorbell is even more exciting than that. Because it's a *magic* doorbell. When it rings, it means there's a magical animal waiting outside our barn. A magical animal who needs our help.

My mom's been helping them basically her whole life. And now *I* get to help, too . . .

CHAPTER 1
BUG HOUSES

A gentle breeze ruffled the tree branches in the forest as I knelt next to my cat. "Now remember, Sassafras—no eating the bugs that come stay in the bug houses we build! They are guests, not food."

"Mrrrowww," grumbled Sassafras.

"Ooh, look, Sass!" I touched a bud on a nearby bush. "The forest roses are getting ready to bloom! Somehow we missed them last year, remember? They sure don't last long."

Sassafras blinked in agreement and came closer to the rose bud. He closed his eyes as he took a big sniff. I leaned my head in next to him and did the same thing.

"Even though we can barely smell them right now, they still smell like the BEST thing in the whole world, don't they? I can't wait until they bloom and the whole forest smells like this!"

I leaned back and set my hand on a fuzzy patch of moss. "Oooh! This will make a perfect carpet for one of our bug houses!"

I peeled it up and continued our walk through the forest, keeping an eye out for sticks, leaves, and lichen—anything that would be good as a part of a bug house. Once my hands were full, I plopped down and got to work building.

"Sass, can you bring me that twig?"

When he brought it over, I gave him a pet and added the twig to cover a gap on one side of the house.

"What kind of bugs do you think will move in? I'm thinking definitely roly-polies with the moss floor. I hope worms move into that pile of dead leaves, and that chunk of wood might get some beetle friends, don't you think?"

Sassafras sniffed a group of leaves nearby, and one wiggled. He bopped it with his paw, and it flipped over.

"Whoa! A little millipede!" He was all curled up so I knew he was scared. I gently set my finger next to him and waited for him to uncurl. He crawled along my finger as I held down a giggle. "He tickles!" I whispered to Sassafras.

I set my finger in the bug house and watched the millipede walk inside. "Make yourself at home, Mr. Millipede!"

Sassafras leaned dangerously close to the millipede but then stopped and shook his head.

I scratched Sassafras under his chin.

"Thank you for being such a good kitty and not trying to snack on our bug friends. I think you've earned some tuna when we get home!"

He purred at the mention of tuna, but then his head snapped to the left and his ears flicked around.

"What is it, Sassafras?" I looked over to where he was staring. "Is it the roses?"

Sassafras chattered, tail puffed up.

I heard a sound like rain, but when I looked up the sky was blue. And when I put my hand out it was dry. "Is it just me or is that sound getting louder?"

Sassafras took a few steps backward, but kept his eyes over by the roses.

I looked again and saw a shadowy cloud moving quickly from rose bush to rose bush. "Weird! It's like a little rain cloud!" I squinted. "Do you think it's making that rain sound, Sassafras?" I looked down at my cat, but he was already gone.

"Oh dear. Always so worried about getting wet." I thought I heard Mom calling me, so I took one last look at the weird shadow cloud and followed Sassafras home.

CHAPTER 2
WHAT WAS THAT?

"Did you make some neat bug houses?" Mom asked as Sassafras and I burst through the back door.

"Yes ... well, no ... well, one, yeah." I plonked down in a chair. "Mom, can tiny rain clouds come down to the ground and rain?"

Mom pulled up a chair. "What makes you ask that?"

"We were building a really great bug house when it started sounding like rain.

There was no rain falling on us, but we spotted a little gray cloud moving through the forest. It freaked Sassafras out."

"Rain clouds don't quite work like that." Mom thought for a minute. "Do you think maybe it could have been a swarm of bugs? Sometimes a group of beating insect wings can sound like rain. When the conditions are just right, you can get several new bugs hatching all at once. And if it was a group of smaller bugs, like gnats, it might have looked like a cloud from far away."

"Oh, that makes sense. Maybe that's what it was," I said as she got up and handed me a snack. "Thanks, Mom." I felt a cat head bump my leg and looked down to see Sassafras staring up at me with big round eyes. "Oh, whoops! I promised you tuna!"

I popped up and grabbed a can and started to open it while Sassafras pranced in circles around his cat dish. The opener stopped, and I turned to give Sassafras his tuna, but he was gone!

"Really, again?" I muttered, but then I heard it. The magic doorbell was ringing!

CHAPTER 3
THINGS
THAT HOP

As I darted through the yard to the barn, I tried to imagine what new magical creature might be waiting for me. A pegasus? A griffin? When I got in the barn, Sassafras was already there waiting for me. I took a single deep breath and opened the door to find ...

"Pip?" My shoulders slumped. It's not that I wasn't excited to see Pip, it's just—I shook it off and knelt down to greet my frog friend.

Pip gave Sassafras a quick hug and started pacing and gesturing. "Zoey, it's the hophops. I can't believe this! Why, oh why did the hophops have to come? And why NOW?!"

"Whoa there, Pip. What happened? And what are hophops?"

Pip stopped and stared at me for a moment. "Oh, right. I always forget how little humans know." He put a webbed hand on his forehead. "OK, so hophops are like . . . the jumpy things that eat a lot?"

Jumpy things? "Ummm, kangaroos?"

"No, no, no. Smaller. You know. Small jumpy things."

"Bunnies? Frogs?"

Pip gave me a look. "Frogs? Really, Zoey?"

We both started laughing. Then Pip got serious again. "Oh, that's right. You call them something like treehops? No. Shrubhops? No, that's not it either." He looked around our yard. "Oh, that's it!

Grassyhops!"

"Grasshoppers?"

Pip clapped his webbed hands together. "Yes! Grasshoppers. Hophops are like the magical version of those, but very small. Usually they just eat a bit here and there—some magical plants and some forest plants. But every once in a while, a big bunch hatches at once and they rush through the forest, eating just about everything in their path."

"Whoa," I said.

"Meow!" said Sassafras.

"I know," said Pip. "So anyway, that's bad and all, but this time it's REALLY, REALLY bad. Because the path they took where they ate everything? Well, it went over a bunch of forest roses."

I swallowed hard. "They ate all the forest roses? But they were just about to bloom." I turned to Sassafras with sad eyes. "We're going to miss them AGAIN this year."

"No . . . well, yes . . . maybe . . ." Pip said and started muttering to himself again.

"I'm so confused, Pip!" I sat down, and Sassafras crawled into my lap and bopped my chin to try to make me feel better.

Pip paused and thought a moment, then grabbed a stick and walked over to a nearby patch of dirt.

"It's like this, Zoey." He drew a round circle with big eyes. "This is a bip."

"A what?" I asked.

He sighed. "Just listen, and it will all make sense. So, as I was saying, this is a bip." Then he drew an arrow and a rose leaf. "This is a forest rose leaf, and that's where allll the bips live. The bips make the forest roses grow." He drew another arrow from the rose leaf and added a rose bloom. Then he added another arrow and sketched something and scribbled it out. And tried again.

Pip muttered some more and sighed. "Well . . . that's close enough. OK, so forest roses are really important because they are the first food of baby hippogriffs."

"BABY HIPPOGRIFFS?!?!" I squealed. I love all baby animals, but magical baby animals are my extra-favorites.

He pointed the stick to the word he'd written. "Baby hippogriffs are born with wings that aren't fully developed. They need the magic from the forest roses to make their wings work."

"AHA!" I cheered. "That's why those roses smell so good—they're magical!" But then I thought about the poor baby hippogriffs, and my smile faded. ""So, without the bips, there won't be roses, and without the roses, the baby hippogriffs won't be able to fly?"

Pip nodded sadly.

"But . . . couldn't they wait until next year to eat next year's roses? Would their wings work then?"

Pip sighed. "Yes, but baby hippogriffs need their wings to escape from predators. Without wings they'd be stuck on the ground, and I don't think many would make it until the next year."

"That's horrible!" I felt tears coming to my eyes. "There must be something we can do to help the babies! Could we feed them regular roses? Or find another magical food or . . . ?"

"No, it *has* to be the magical forest roses. That's why we need you to save them!"

"But I thought the hophops ate all of them?"

"No, the hophops ate all the bips on the roses," Pip said. "I think the bips saved the roses, actually. The hophops move pretty quickly through the forest so they must've just gotten to the bips before they moved on. They didn't eat any of the rose buds or leaves."

"Oh, phew!" My shoulders relaxed a bit.

"But even though the roses are still here, they are starting to die without the bips. Zoey, you have to find a way to get more bips—and FAST!"

More bips. Quickly. No problem. Now I just needed to, you know, figure out what they were.

CHAPTER 4
LOOKY THINGY

"What are you waiting for? Grab your Looky Thingy and let's go!" Pip put his hands on his hips and tapped his foot.

"Erm, my Looky Thingy?" I asked.

Pip nodded. "Bips are quite small and hard to see."

"Uh, so a microscope?" I guessed.

Pip sighed. "No, you can just bring your Looky Thingy that makes things bigger. You know?" He made a circle with his hands and peeked one eye through.

"Ohhhh, a magnifying glass! Let me go tell Mom where I'm going and grab it from the house." As I ran inside, Pip muttered something about human words for things.

I let Mom know what was happening while I looked through my room. "Oh gosh, those poor baby hippogriffs!" Mom said as she lifted my bed quilt to reveal my magnifying glass.

"Thanks, Mom!" I gave her a quick hug.

"I hope we can find a way to get more bips and save the roses in time."

"If anyone can do it, it's you, sweetheart." She kissed my forehead and handed me my backpack. "I'll stay here so Dad doesn't wonder where we are when he gets back from his errands, but let me know if you need any help."

"I will!" I hollered over my shoulder and ran back to the barn.

Sassafras and I followed Pip into the forest, and he explained a little more. "This morning, we were playing a game of tag, and one of my friends saw the hophop path with everything eaten. We followed part of it through the forest and saw the sick roses all along the way. We grabbed our Looky Thingies and checked and couldn't see any bips on the rose leaves. I sent my friends to go see if the hophop path missed any forest roses. We're all going to meet up by the stream."

I crossed my fingers that the other

frogs had found some healthy roses with bips.

"Wait here," Pip instructed when we got to the stream. "I'm sure you remember that most magical creatures are really shy."

I nodded, and Sassafras meowed.

"I just need to let my friends know that it's you guys, so they don't freak out. Once I call you over, just remember to walk really slowly and use a quiet voice, OK? Forest frogs get scared easily."

Sassafras and I sat down on a log to wait as Pip hopped ahead.

CHAPTER 5
FOREST FROGS

"OK, you can come over now, Zoey and Sassafras!" Pip hollered from a few feet away.

"Ready?" I whispered to Sassafras.

"Meow," he whispered back.

We crept slowly over to where Pip was standing with a group of five little forest frogs of various bright colors. I squatted down so I wouldn't look super tall to them and gave a slow wave. Two of them waved back, but the other three looked down at

their feet. So shy!

Pip cleared his throat. "So, the news isn't great. My friends followed the mess the hophops left, and most of the forest roses had all of their bips eaten." Pip pointed over to his right, and I turned to look.

"WHOOOOOAAAA!" I shouted.

"Eeeep!" squealed the tiniest frog, and he hopped behind a rock and hid.

"Oh gosh, sorry!" I whispered. "I didn't
mean to shout. I just hadn't seen the
damage from the hophops yet. Pip, you
weren't kidding when you said they ate
just about everything in their path!"

Over where Pip had pointed was a
path several feet wide that stretched way
back into the forest. In the path were a few
nubs of grasses and some wilty, pale forest
roses . . . and dirt. Just about everything

else had been eaten up.

I stood on my tippy-toes and tried to follow the path through the forest. "Ohhhhh," I said under my breath. The path twisted around over to where Sassafras and I had been building Bug Houses yesterday.

"Hey, Pip? Do the hophops look like a gray cloud?"

"Only sometimes. Usually just a few here or there are nibbling on plants. Not enough to be more than a bother. But every few years we get too many hatching all at once. And this happens." He poked at the dirt left behind and sighed, and then he hopped over to a wilty-looking forest rose. "Bring your Looky Thingy and look here."

I peered through the magnifying glass at the leaf Pip pointed to. "It looks neat up close like this," I said as I tilted the magnifying glass and leaf for Sassafras to take a peek.

Pip sighed. "Right, but it also has no
bips. That's not good."

"Uhh, what do bips look like exactly?
Are they usually on the leaves?" I asked.

"Over here!" squeaked a faraway frog
voice.

Sass and I followed Pip over to his
friend who was standing by a single,
healthy forest rose bush.

"I finally found one!" She pointed at

the bright rose bush. "This is what it's supposed to look like when you look through your Looky Thingy."

"Oh my goodness!" I whispered. "Sassafras! Look!" I tilted the leaf and magnifying glass down for Sass, and he touched his nose to it. "Oh gosh, bips are really, really cute."

I bent down by Sassafras and watched them all. Instead of seeing the leaf surface with all of its veins, this rose leaf looked like a sea of miniature green creatures. They wiggled this way and that as they looked up at us with their eyes.

I noticed that one bip in particular was moving a lot, and then there seemed to be a spark of light. "Did you see that?" I rubbed my eyes before looking back through my magnifying glass. "Oh, wow. I was sure that was just one bip a second ago, but now there are two!"

Pip leaned over to look. "Hm, I just see a lot of bips!"

"Oh! What if we took some of these bips and put them on the other roses? Do you think that could fix them?"

"That wouldn't work," Pip replied. "Do you see how many there are? The forest roses need strong magic to help the baby hippogriff wings work. We'd need hundreds ... no, thousands ... no, bazillions of bips to make the magic that strong in the roses. If we took some from this one, then neither rose would have enough." Pip flopped down and put his head in his hands.

"Those poor baby hippogriffs." One of the frogs sobbed and started to cry.

Pip hopped over and put his arm around his friend. "Don't worry, Zoey will figure this out. She'll fix it!"

Right, I thought to myself. Zoey will fix this ... somehow.

CHAPTER 6
A PLAN

All of the frogs looked up at me hopefully.

I took some deep breaths. I needed a plan. I also needed my Thinking Goggles—which of course I forgot in my hurry!

I took off my backpack and opened it to put my magnifying glass away when I spotted my Thinking Goggles.

"Thanks, Mom!" I whispered. She must have put them in my backpack while I was looking for my magnifying glass.

I popped the Thinking Goggles on my head and started walking slowly in a little circle and talking to myself. Sassafras and the little group of forest frogs watched me curiously.

"OK, so we know we can't just spread out the bips that are left. We need a lot more bips. . . . a bazillion bips . . ." I tapped my Thinking Goggles. "A bazillion bips to replace all the bips that the bazillion hophops ate. Wait. Hophops! So many hophops! That's it! We need a SWARM of bips!" I cheered.

I knelt down by Pip. "I was asking Mom about the cloud of things we saw yesterday in the forest—it must have been the hophops. Mom said when everything is just right, you can sometimes get a big swarm or cloud of bugs because a bunch of them hatch all at once."

"That makes sense," Pip said.

"So, that's what we need to do with the bips! We need to figure out how to make everything just right for them and grow a big bunch all at once!"

Pip grinned. "That sounds like a perfect plan, Zoey!"

I smiled back and then gulped. "Errrm, we just need to figure out the perfect conditions for bips to grow. You guys wouldn't happen to know that, would you?"

The frogs all looked at each other and shook their heads.

One of the frogs started to cry again. "This will never work. The hippogriff eggs are about to hatch. We don't have any time!"

My stomach flipped. "Pip, is that true? Are the eggs ready to hatch now?"

"I only know that they'll hatch soon." Pip thought for a moment. "We probably ought to visit a hippogriff nest and find out for sure."

I clapped my hands over my mouth so I wouldn't squeal and scare the frogs. A hippogriff nest!

CHAPTER 7
HOW LONG?

We hiked a long way to a large gathering of rocks. Pip stopped at the bottom and turned to me and Sassafras. "Magical creatures are usually really shy. Hippogriffs are some of the shyest forest creatures and they are very protective of their nests. You guys can come, but stay really far back and stay low to the ground. And be VERY quiet, OK?"

I nodded and Sass purred in reply.

We scrabbled up the rock. Luckily,

Sassafras was able to hop from one little ledge to another and follow us up. Once we got to the top, Pip held up a webbed hand to motion for us to stop. Sassafras and I stayed on our bellies as Pip hopped over to a HUGE nest of sticks and branches.

Pip coughed quietly and then called out gently, "Um, hello there, hippogriffs? Just Pip here, a friendly forest frog."

I gasped and Sass pressed himself

further into the rock when a large eagle
head popped out of the nest and watched
Pip hop closer.

"Oh, uh . . . hello, sir," Pip said. "There's
been a slight problem with the bips
and the forest roses. The hophops came
through and ate most of the bips . . ."

The eagle head shrieked in reply.

All of Sassafras' fur immediately
poofed out. I reached over and put a

calming hand on him.

"I know, I know." Pip shook his head. "My friends Zoey and Sassafras and I are all working on fixing it right now. We were just wondering—how long do you think before the eggs start hatching?"

The eagle head disappeared into the nest, and we heard some rustling. It reappeared and the hippogriff shrieked again.

Pip gulped. "In that case, we'd better hurry. Thank you, sir!"

As Pip turned and hopped over to us, a giant shadow glided over the rock. All

three of us looked over in time to watch
the hippogriff mama land in the nest. The
dad and mom spoke back and forth in
eagle calls. For a full minute, none of us
said anything because we could only stare
at the enormous and beautiful hippogriffs.

I felt a webbed hand on mine and
looked over to see Pip looking worried.
"He says three days, maybe four before
the eggs start hatching. Is it enough time,
Zoey?"

Three or four days? My stomach did
another flip. It would have to be enough.

CHAPTER 8

EXPERIMENTS!

"I need to get home to Mom and my science journal, but let's think while we jog back." I puffed as Pip, Sassafras, and I all hurried. "Right now, the normal forest environment makes bips grow at a normal speed, but I need to find a way to make them super happy so they will grow super fast."

I leapt over a fallen log. "I need to change only one thing in an experiment at a time," I continued, "but I also need to try different things. That means I need to run a few experiments. And we don't have much time . . . so I should try to set them up all at once!"

"All I know is that bips need roses," said Pip. "I've never seen them anywhere else."

"OK, good." I hopped across a series of rocks. "What else do we know? Oh—they're green like a plant! Plants need sunlight, so I should try one experiment with light."

"Do you think they're a kind of tiny plant?" Pip asked.

"Good question. I mean, they're green, but they also had eyes, and I was pretty sure I saw them moving a bit . . . maybe some kind of plant-like bacteria?" I guessed as we burst through the trees and into my backyard. "Let's ask Mom!"

Pip hopped onto my head, and we all crashed through the back door into the kitchen. I tossed my backpack to the side and kicked off my muddy shoes, calling out, "Moooooom!"

Pip leapt from my head and gave my mom's cheek a hug, and Mom kissed his head. "What did you guys find out?"

I grabbed my science journal and a pencil and we all sat down at the kitchen table. I told Mom what we knew so far about the bips, how I'd need to run some experiments to see if I could get more bips to grow, and how we only had a few days left to figure it out.

"Oh my, in that case—let's get started!"

Mom said. "So, if bips are a kind of photosynthetic bacteria, what do you think they might need, Zoey?"

"Photo-syn-thetic," I said slowly and then smiled. "That's the word you use when you're talking about how plants make their own food from the sun, right?"

Mom grinned and nodded.

"OK," I said, "we should definitely do an experiment with sunlight. And if they might be a kind of bacteria, sometimes warming bacteria can make them grow faster . . . so maybe an experiment with temperature?" I wrote both ideas down in my journal.

"Those sound great," said Mom. "Can you think of one more you might want to try . . . ?"

"Hmmm . . ." I tapped my Thinking Goggles. "Maybe water or . . . um, moisture? Because all living things need water?"

"It sounds like you've got the

experiment ideas covered. How about
some help with materials?" Mom grabbed
some large plastic containers from a
kitchen drawer and set them on the table.
"Do these look like they'll work?"

"Those are perfect!" I paused to think.
"Mom? So far, we've only found one
healthy rose. I don't want to take too many
bips from it because it might get sick too.
How many do you think I should use? If I
take one leaf's worth for each experiment
from different rose bushes, do you think

that will be OK?"

Mom looked at Pip. "What do you think?"

"It sounds like we need to find some more healthy roses," Pip said. "I'll get my frog friends to scout the forest this evening, and then come back tomorrow morning and let you know if there are others."

"Thank you, Pip!" I blew out a deep breath. There just had to be more healthy roses somewhere. I gave Pip a gentle hug goodbye and went back to writing out the three experiments in my science journal.

CHAPTER 9
SO MANY EXPERIMENTS!

Sassafras shifted in my lap, and I reached down to scratch under his chin. "I think I have all of this in order, Sass, but let me read it out loud to make sure."

I flipped back to the first of the three experiments I had written down—the water experiment—and read the question to Sassafras:

How much water do bips need?

Sassafras meowed.

"Good, I'm glad you agree." I moved my hand to scratch behind his left ear. "Next up: hypothesis. I think the bips will multiply the fastest on the napkin that gets four sprays."

Sassafras purred.

Next I read him the materials list:

MATERIALS:
Large plastic container
Napkins
Masking tape
Permanent marker
Spray bottle
water
Bips

Sassafras bumped his head against the science journal, still purring.

"Next up—procedure!" I read each of the steps aloud to him.

1. Place three napkins on the bottom of the container with space between them.

2. Place a tape label with the number of sprays by each napkin.

3. Spray two sprays of water on the napkin labeled 2, four sprays on 4, and six sprays on 6.

Sassafras sat up and meowed.

"I didn't have to do zero sprays because we know all living things need water," I replied.

Sassafras blinked once and then lay back down.

I continued reading:

4. Add a leaf full of bips to the center of the container.

5. Cover the container with plastic wrap and poke holes for air.

6. Check on the bips every two hours and record the number of bips on each napkin.

I paused. "Mom?" I hollered.

Once she came over I asked, "I shouldn't leave the bips for more than a day, right? Since they're living things and I don't really know what they eat and all that…"

Mom patted my head. "Smart thinking! In my experience most magical creatures grow pretty quickly, so hopefully you'll have some results in a few hours. But I agree, it's safest to return the bips to the forest roses at the end of the day."

I added one more step:

7. After one day, return the bips to the forest rose they were taken from.

I had created a data chart that would

be all ready to fill in, but it would be hard to read that out loud to Sassafras. So, I looked it over myself again and added some lines to make it easier to fill in later.

RESULTS:

Starting number of bips: _____

	Number of bips	After 2 hours	After 4 hours	After 6 hours	After 8 hours
2 spray napkin					
4 spray napkin					
6 spray napkin					

I'd left space for my conclusion, which was perfect. I took a breath and then flipped to the next page to start reading the next experiment aloud.

Dad cleared his throat, and I jumped. "Whoa! Sorry, Dad—I didn't even see you there!" I was so busy I hadn't noticed the whole kitchen table was filled with dinner food.

"I know you're probably busy saving the world with science," Dad chuckled, "but even scientists need to eat."

Mom winked at me, and I grinned. Dad had no idea because he doesn't know about the magical creatures (he can't see them), but I kind of *was* working on saving the world. Well, saving the baby hippogriffs at least!

After dinner Mom let me stay up a bit past my bedtime, so I managed to write up all four experiments. As I fell asleep, I reminded myself that everything was ready to go the next morning for a full day of science.

CHAPTER 10
BIP GATHERING

"Remember to breathe!" Mom joked as Sassafras and I hurried through our breakfasts.

I took one last gulp of water and stood up. "Ready!"

Sassafras came over still chewing a mouthful of cat food, and I gathered up all my supplies.

Mom tapped my science journal. "I'll be sure the materials are set up in the barn for you when you get back."

"Thank you, Mom!"

We ran out the back door . . . and nearly crashed into a yawning Pip.

I skidded to a stop. "Good news?" I held my breath.

Pip stretched and then grinned. "My friends found four other healthy roses."

"Yes!" I pumped my fist. "That should be perfect."

Once we arrived, I used my scissors to clip one leaf from each healthy rose.

Pip rubbed his eyes. "I thought you were doing three experiments—why are you clipping four leaves?"

"I'm getting one leaf for each experiment," I replied, "and the fourth leaf will be in a container by itself, so I'll have an idea how quickly bips usually multiply. That way I can compare it to my experiments to make sure they're creating more bips than if I'd done nothing at all."

"Ohhhh, that makes sense," Pip said.

Once we had the leaves, we rushed back to the barn. Mom had set up everything for me, so I was ready to go! One small table had a water bottle and napkins for my water experiment. Another table was scootched over to the wall—Mom had set up a heating pad next to a big glass container. On the last table, a large container sat under two grow lights that we used each year to get our garden sprouts ready. They even had timers on them! I was so glad, because the sunlight experiment would've been hard to do without them.

"Thank you, Mom! This is all so perfect," I said, and then dove right into setting up my experiments by following the procedures I'd written out in my science journal.

Next, I got out my magnifying glass and started counting bips. I recorded the numbers in the different data charts in my journal. Each leaf had a different number, but they all had around 200 bips on them.

Once all the experiments were set up, I looked at the clock. 8:00 a.m. Not bad! I set a two-hour timer, and Pip and Sassafras and I went to the garden to explore and play until it was time to record my first results.

CHAPTER 11

RESULTS

"Knock knock." Mom opened the barn door. "How's it coming along out here? I thought I'd come check on you guys while Dad makes dinner."

I rubbed my face. "It's going OK." I pointed to the container with just the bips on the rose leaf and flipped to that chart in my science journal. "This one started the day with 223 bips, and the last count I did had it up to 231."

I sat down and flipped to the next page

in my journal. "For the water experiment, most of the bips were huddled on the four-spray napkin—the total number of bips in that experiment went from 213 this morning to 284."

"That's a good sign," Mom said.

"I figured something else out with that one." I waved her over to the water experiment and handed her the magnifying glass. "You kinda have to wait for a minute and make sure you're really quiet."

"What am I looking for?" Mom asked.

"Just wait a few minutes—you'll know it when you see it." I held a finger up to my lips to remind Sass to be extra quiet.

Mom peered into the container, and then she gave a little jump and started laughing. "Did . . . did that bip just burp?"

I couldn't help laughing again. "I'm pretty sure it did. Do you think it's burping some kind of light? It's SO bright, right?"

"It really is—it surprised me! And yes, that does seem like a really strong light to me."

"It must be a way they help the roses, don't you think? And I'm pretty sure they're called bips because they make that little 'bip' noise as they burp. Did you hear it?"

Mom started cracking up again.

"Bips burp light!" I laughed. Then I sighed. It was an interesting finding, but it really didn't get us any closer to figuring out how to grow a ton of bips all at once. I flipped to another experiment. "Speaking of light, with the sunlight experiment, the bips all moved to be right under the grow light that stayed on all day. In that container, the number of bips went from 189 bips in the morning to 301 when I just counted."

"OK, so the sunlight seems to help."

"But the temperature experiment didn't really seem to do anything. I set it up with an unheated side and a heated side, but they were spread out all over the container. And the total number of bips just went from 221 to 228—not a big change."

I smooshed my hands down my cheeks. "The water and the sunlight made some difference, but not like a crazy amount. I just don't think I can grow enough bips in time to save the baby hippogriffs. Plus, I need to return the ones I have to the forest, right? I've had them for the full day."

Mom looked through my journal. "Well, it seems like you are making them happy enough with the water and sunlight. I think it would be safe to keep them overnight. Do you want to combine the things that have been successful into one environment for them to stay in until tomorrow morning?"

"If you think they'll be all right, that would be great. I'm kind of tired from counting bips all day." I yawned and stretched. "So maybe I'll put all the rose leaves in a container, spray each section in there four times with water, and switch the grow lights so that they stay on all night?"

"That sounds like a great plan. But try

to hurry because Dad's almost done with dinner!"

Once I got them all set up in their new home under the grow light, I gave the container a little hug and whispered, "Grow, bips, grow!"

CHAPTER 12
BEDTIME

I flumped down on my bed with a big dramatic sigh. "I just feel like I'm missing something, Mom. Can you think of anything else I could try with the bips?"

Mom tapped her chin. "Let's both sleep on it. Maybe something will come to us overnight. Speaking of which, wait here!"

I heard her rustling through the hall closet, and she reappeared with both hands behind her back.

"You're being weird, Mom." I giggled.

"I was going to save this for the next holiday, but you might need it tonight," she said, and she brought out her hands to reveal what she'd been hiding.

A new bonnet! "Whoaaaa, are those Thinking Goggles?!" I ran my hands over the satin fabric that was covered in drawings of science goggles.

"Mmm-hmm." Mom nodded proudly. "When Dad saw this fabric, we knew you had to have it! Who knows, maybe your Thinking Goggles bonnet will give you ideas in your dreams."

I gave her a big hug and hollered out, "Thank you, Dad!"

I pulled the bonnet down over my curls and nestled down into bed. I thought I could feel some tingling—just like when my Thinking Goggles were giving me an idea.

"What am I missing with the bips?" I whispered over and over until I fell asleep.

CHAPTER 13
DREAM HIKE

"That's it!" I shouted as I rocketed out of bed the next morning.

Poor Sassafras flew into the air and landed at my feet with big wide eyes. All of his fur was fluffed out to the max.

"Oh, sorry, buddy!" I gave him a gentle pet. "This new bonnet worked just like my Thinking Goggles. I had a dream, and I think I figured out what I've been missing. At least, sort of. Let's go get Mom!"

I burst into the kitchen to find Dad

making pancakes and Mom setting the table.

"Any thoughts come to you as you slept?" asked Mom.

"Yes!" I cheered. "I dreamed we were all hiking in the forest, and I found some really cool lichen that looked like dragon scales."

"Oh, I love that kind of lichen," Dad chimed in.

"It's my favorite kind." I nodded. "Anyway, Mom you were telling me in my dream how lichen is special. How it's really two things working together, right? A fungus and, uh, a . . . ?"

"Alga," Mom added.

"Right. And you said it's a special relationship because the alga makes food by photosynthesis—like a plant, right? And it shares some of that food with the fungus. And the fungus is like the house that the alga lives in? And it shares water and vitamin-stuff with the alga?"

"Good memory!" Mom said as she gave me two pancakes.

"So, I was thinking about that, uh . . . " I glanced at Dad, "*story* we were talking about yesterday with the bips and the roses. That maybe it was sort of like the lichen—where the bips give the roses something, and the roses give the bips something. And I was thinking the bips give the roses a boost of sunlight with their, um, burps?"

Dad raised an eyebrow at me. "Burping bips?" He started laughing. "You two definitely have fantastic imaginations!"

Mom winked at me. "Yes, we do! And Zoey, I think you could be right. What do you think the roses give the bips, though?"

"Right. That's where I'm stuck." I sighed dramatically.

"Can I help tell the story?" Dad asked, and Mom and I nodded. "In that case,

obviously the roses could contribute their smell. I mean, who doesn't love the scent of roses?" Dad chuckled. "If I were a bip, I'd definitely make my home on a delicious-smelling rose."

Smell! I hadn't tried a smell experiment yet—maybe there was something super tiny in good smells that helped the bips grow! "Dad, you're a genius!" I shouted and jumped up and started toward the barn.

Dad patted my chair. "Zoey, you might want to finish your breakfast before you go off and play."

"Oh, right." I sat down and ate the rest of my pancakes as I thought about the smell experiment. I could try vanilla and chocolate and orange and rose, of course. We had vanilla extract and cocoa powder in the kitchen cabinet. I looked around the kitchen and spotted oranges on the counter. But what about roses?

"OH NOOOO," I groaned.

Dad put a hand to my forehead. "Are

you feeling OK, sweetie? You're acting kind of strange this morning."

"Sorry, Dad. I'm, uh, running a pretend experiment in the barn with the bips, and I wanted to try your idea of the rose smell with them, but we don't have any roses in the forest yet, and I don't know how to make a rose scent with stuff from our house."

Dad looked over at Mom. "Didn't someone give you rose oil as a gift a few years ago?"

"That's right!" Mom said. She ate her last bite of pancake and stood up. "I'll go get the bottle for you right now."

In no time at all, I headed out to the barn with Sassafras and my arms full of supplies to run a scent experiment.

CHAPTER 14
THE FIFTH EXPERIMENT

I set down all of my supplies, and I'd started to set up the container when Sassafras meowed and pawed at my science journal.

"Good thinking, Sassafras." I ruffled his fur. "It won't take too long to write this down, and then I'll remember what I did."

I started with my question:

Does a certain scent make more bips?

HYPOTHESIS:

I think the rose oil will make more bips.

I listed my materials and then moved on to my procedure:

1. Put five labeled cotton balls spaced apart in a big container.

2. Measure one teaspoon of vanilla extract and pour it onto one of the cotton balls.

3. Measure one teaspoon of cocoa powder mixed with a little water and pour it onto another cotton ball.

4. Squeeze 1 teaspoon of orange juice and pour it onto another cotton ball.

5. Measure 1 teaspoon of rose oil and pour it onto a fourth cotton ball.

6. Leave the last cotton ball plain.

7. Add 200 bips to the center of the container.

8. Put a plastic wrap lid over the top of the container and poke air holes in it.

9. Check the number of bips on each cotton ball every two hours.

I counted out 200 bips and put the lid on the container. "Please, please, please work," I whispered to the experiment. Then I opened the barn door to find Pip about to ring the doorbell.

"Zoey! The first of the healthy forest roses is blooming. I checked with the hippogriff parents in the area, and they think the eggs will hatch later today or tomorrow. Have you figured it out?"

It felt like I swallowed a rock. "Um, not yet Pip."

His shoulders fell, and he looked at the ground. "But . . . it's *time*."

"I know." I blinked quickly. I didn't want to start crying. I needed a distraction. "Here, I'll show you my newest experiment. Hopefully it will do the trick?"

Pip followed me into the barn, and all three of us skidded to a stop.

"Whooooaaaa!" Pip said. "Is it supposed to be doing that?"

The container with the smells was erupting with lots of quiet little *bips* and bursts of light were popping out like firecrackers.

Sassafras stayed far away with his tail puffed, but Pip and I ran over to get a closer look.

"Sheesh, I could really use some sunglasses!" I narrowed my eyes to see where all the bips were. There were a few bipping over on the vanilla extract cotton ball. But a big pile of them were bipping away on the rose oil cotton ball.

Wait. A big PILE?

"PIP!!! That's soooo many more bips than were there a few minutes ago. It's working! Something in the rose oil is helping make a ton more bips!"

Pip squinted and got down by the rose-scented cotton ball. He sniffed. "This doesn't smell nearly as good as a forest rose. Do you think if we got one of the real rose blooms, it would work even better?"

I thought for just a moment. "Yeah, I really do. But can we take a rose? I mean, we're already so short on roses for the baby hippogriffs that will be here any minute."

"I know," Pip said, "but if this fixes all the forest roses, there will be plenty, right?"

"True. OK, let's do it. But first I need to let Mom know where we're going."

"Hurry, Zoey!" Pip called as I dashed to the house.

CHAPTER 15
OUR LAST HOPE

I cradled the forest rose blossom in my hands on our way back to the barn.

"You're right, Pip, this does smell a billion times better than the perfume." I took a deep breath. "It's basically the best smell in the world."

Sassafras chattered in agreement.

I walked around a patch of squishy mud. "So, I was thinking, what if I use whole petals instead of mashing them up and squeezing the oil onto cotton balls?

That way, if this doesn't work, we could still feed it to a baby hippogriff."

"It's going to work. It's got to! But that's good thinking," Pip said.

I opened the barn door and saw Mom inside. She was setting up a giant container with all the bips we had so far, making sure the sunlight and water level matched what had been successful with my experiments.

Mom turned to me and handed me a pair of sunglasses. "Just in case this works as well as we think it might." She put some on herself. Then she gave Pip and Sassafras a pair of Dad's sunglasses, and they squished together behind the glasses.

"Come on, forest rose," I said, and I placed it in the center of the container near a small group of bips.

Sounds of *bip bip bip bip bip* filled the barn! Spurts of light filled the container ... and the container filled with bips.

"YESSSS!!!!" we all shouted at once.

Pip gave me a hug. "Just in time, Zoey! You did it!"

"We all did it!" I said and hugged him back.

"Let's get these bips to the forest!" Mom said and passed us each some smaller containers. She even had a tiny waist pack so Sassafras could help carry them. We gently scooped as many bips as we could fit into our containers and headed to the forest.

CHAPTER 16

BUT WHAT ABOUT . . . ?

The four of us huddled together and watched in awe. We'd poured about one container full of bips on each of the wilted forest roses we could find, and right before our eyes the droopy, gray rose bushes sparked to life with the quiet *bip bip bip* sounds of thousands of bips.

Buds that had started to shrivel in the last few days plumped up.

Then they slowly started to open.

"Woooooooooowww," we all breathed.

Sassafras couldn't help but purr.

I looked down at Pip with a smile, but noticed that Pip was looking behind us with a frown.

"What's wrong?" I asked.

"Well, this is super great," he said, "but I'm just wondering, what about all the other dying forest roses?" He pointed down the long dirt path the hophops had taken to get here. "They ate bips off all the roses for miles and miles and miles.

We couldn't get to all of them in time for the baby hippogriffs' hatching. It's too far to hike, and your mom can't drive in the forest, so . . ." He shrugged sadly.

"Well . . . we could get as many as possible. It's early in the day. I'm a good hiker . . . I mean, we could at least get to some?"

"Yeah." Pip shrugged. "I guess we can just try our best to fix it and it'll help some of the baby hippogriffs. I just wish there was a way to help all of them."

"If only we could fly." I sighed.

"Ohhhhhhhh!" Mom and I said at the same time while Sassafras let out a big "MEOW!"

Pip looked around at all of us. "Huh?"

"MARSHMALLOW!" I cheered.

"YES!" Pip gave me a high-five.

But then I paused. "Pip? How can we find him? We haven't seen him since he was a baby."

"Let me worry about that. He could

be anywhere, but forest frogs live all throughout the forest. If I send word out that it's a baby hippogriff emergency, a frog somewhere should be able to find him." Pip had started pacing, but now he stopped and turned to us. "You three head back to the barn and make as many bips as you possibly can. Get ready for an airborne delivery to all the sick forest roses!"

"Should I grab a few more forest roses

since we need to make buckets of bips?" I asked Mom.

"Definitely. And buckets . . . that's a good idea. I wonder if we can make dragon-sized saddlebags out of trash cans and rope . . . hmmm . . ."

Mom headed back to the barn while Sassafras and I took three more forest roses—each from a different forest rose bush. And before leaving for the barn with Sassafras, I took one moment with my eyes closed to breathe in the magical smell of all of those roses at once.

CHAPTER 17
DING DONG

Mom and I set up some old garbage cans with sunlight, water, and one forest rose each. Thank goodness for sunglasses—our whole barn was lit up with bip burps.

When the magic doorbell rang, it took only a millisecond for me to fling the door open.

"MARSHMALLOW!" I squealed. "You're HUGE!"

I could hardly believe it. My baby dragon was back, and he was enormous.

Almost as big as my friend Tiny!

Marshmallow leaned his head down, and I wrapped my arms around part of his giant neck and gave him a hug. He leaned his head even further down, and Sassafras purred as he and Marshmallow gently bopped their heads together.

"Everyone ready?" called a frog voice.

Pip hopped down from Marshmallow's back, and I covered a giggle. With his scarf and goggles, he looked like a tiny frog airplane pilot!

"I'm going to fly on Marshmallow and direct him to the different roses. Do you have a container or scooper for me to pour out the bips?"

We heard a dragging sound behind us and Mom appeared, pulling four large garbage cans that had rope between them. She gave one of Marshmallow's tree-trunk legs a hug, and then hurried over to hand Pip a plastic cup that was almost as big as him. "Can you lift that, or is it too big?"

Pip grinned and held it over his head. "No problem."

Mom turned to me next. "OK, Zoey. I need your help lifting these up onto Marshmallow. Thankfully the bips aren't too heavy."

Pip went over to

Marshmallow and made some hand gestures. Marshmallow lay down on his stomach and stretched his neck out flat along the ground. Mom and I set it up so that two garbage cans full of bips were on each side of Marshmallow, with the ropes running between them across his back.

"Good luck!" Mom and I cheered as Marshmallow beat his giant wings and he and Pip took off for the forest.

About an hour later they returned with empty cans.

"It worked!" Pip cheered. "We could see the forest roses sparking back to life from the air. It was incredible. And not a moment too soon. We spotted a few hippogriffs hatching as we flew." Pip took off his scarf and goggles and wiped his forehead. "Now remember, hippogriffs are very shy, and *very* protective of their babies . . . but if you all can be very, very quiet, I know where we can probably see a baby hippogriff eating its first meal of forest roses."

CHAPTER 18

IT'S TIME!

Marshmallow was surprisingly silent moving through the forest—and somehow he could weave between the trees despite his enormous size.

"Shhhh," Pip reminded us once we caught up to him. He pointed to a log, and Sassafras, Mom, and I silently squatted down behind it. Marshmallow stopped by some trees and started shimmering. I rubbed my eyes. I could barely see him— his scales shifted to the same colors as the trees behind him.

Mom tapped me and pointed at two proud hippogriff parents nudging a tiny wobbly baby forward. The baby hippogriff took a few toddling steps and tumbled over. It let out a little tiny eagle shriek. The dad hippogriff came over and gave it a gentle head bump, and the baby huffed as it got to its feet again. It tottered over to a forest rose and gobbled it down. Its little wings wiggled and sparkled and . . . grew a tiny bit.

"Whoaaaa," I whispered.

Pip glared at me, and I put a hand over my mouth. He nodded once, and we both looked back over at the baby who had toddled to another rose bloom.

I felt my chest swell with pride. All the rose bushes in this clearing were completely healthy—and completely covered in delicious-smelling rose blooms.

Once the baby gobbled a second bloom, its wings shook again, grew a bit more, and then started beating faster and faster. After it ate a third rose, the baby flew up into the air! The parents gave a cry and started flying off toward the mountains, and the baby gave a tiny cry in return and followed.

Their beating wings blew a single rose petal over to our log.

I picked it up and sniffed. "This would be so cool to keep in my science journal," I said, but then I sighed and put it back on the forest floor. "I'll leave it for the baby hippogriffs, though."

Pip picked it up and handed it to me. "Thanks to you, there are plenty of forest roses now. You should keep this one."

I looked over at Mom and she nodded.

We said our thank-yous and goodbyes to Marshmallow and Pip—after all that work delivering the bips they were both exhausted, but oh so proud.

As soon as we got home, I pressed the rose petal into my science journal right after the pages on bip experiments. I flipped the page and piled some books on the left side of my journal to help press and preserve the magical forest rose petal. The right side of my science journal was open to a new blank page, ready for the next magical creature we would meet.

GLOSSARY

Algae: Plantlike things that have chlorophyll (for photosynthesis!) but don't have true stems, roots, or leaves (so they're not plants even though they can look like them).

Bacteria: Tiny microscopic living things that can be helpful or harmful, depending on the type.

Data: Information about your experiment that you write down. Data can be measurements or observations.

Fungus: A living thing that is neither a plant nor an animal. A mushroom is a kind of fungus.

Grow light: A special kind of lamp or bulb that makes light similar to sunlight so you can grow plants inside.

Lichen: A living thing made up of alga or cyanobacteria living alongside fungus in a special relationship. You can usually find it growing on trees and rocks in forests.

Photosynthesis: The process by which green plants use sunlight to make their own food.

ABOUT THE AUTHOR AND ILLUSTRATOR

ASIA CITRO used to be a science teacher, but now she plays at home with her two kids and writes books. When she was little, she had a cat just like Sassafras. He loved to eat bugs and always made her laugh (his favorite toy was a plastic human nose that he carried everywhere). Asia has also written three activity books: *150+ Screen-Free Activities for Kids, The Curious Kid's Science Book,* and *A Little Bit of Dirt.* She has yet to find a baby dragon in her backyard, but she always keeps an eye out, just in case.

MARION LINDSAY is a children's book illustrator who loves stories and knows a good one when she reads it. She likes to draw anything and everything but does spend a completely unfair amount of time drawing cats. Sometimes she has to draw dogs just to make up for it. She illustrates picture books and chapter books as well as painting paintings and designing patterns. Like Asia, Marion is always on the lookout for dragons and sometimes thinks there might be a small one living in the airing cupboard.

for activities and more visit
ZOEYANDSASSAFRAS.COM